To Nicole, David, Natalie, Liliana, and Keaton
—W. S.

To teachers—who invest their talents, energy, and compassion in our future
—L. H.

two lions

Text copyright © 2021 by Wendi Silvano
Illustrations copyright © 2021 by Lee Harper
All rights reserved.

Published by Two Lions, New York
www.apub.com
Amazon, the Amazon logo, and Two Lions are trademarks of Amazon.com, Inc., or its affiliates.
ISBN-13: 9781542023641
ISBN-10: 1542023645

The illustrations were rendered in watercolor and pencil on Arches hot press watercolor paper.
Book design by Tanya Ross-Hughes
Printed in China
First Edition
10 9 8 7 6 5 4 3 2 1

Turkey
Goes to School

by
Wendi Silvano

illustrated by
Lee Harper

The first day of school was fast approaching.
Max and Millie were superexcited.

And so were the animals on Farmer Jake's farm—especially
since the first week's theme was "Farm Days."

They were certain they would be invited.

"Stories, counting, singing, painting . . . ," said Turkey.
"It all sounds so fun!
I can't wait to go!"

Each day Turkey got his pals to practice their school skills so they'd be ready.
They wrote their names . . .

counted corn kernels . . .

read stories . . .

and even tried out recess games.

But when the big day came they were booted off the bus.

"Critters aren't allowed at school," said Millie.
"You need to stay at the farm."

"Gobble, gobble," groaned Turkey. "We just have to go to school.
We can't miss out on all that fun!"

"Well then," said Horse.
"Let's giddyap and GO!"

When the animals arrived, teachers were talking.
Children were chasing. Parents were taking pictures.

"It's too **b-a-a-a-d** critters aren't allowed in class," said Sheep.

"It's total **hogwash**," grunted Pig. "Turkey, why don't we team up
to sneak you in . . . and then maybe you can get us in."

"**Gobbledy-good** idea!" said Turkey. "I think I know just what to do. No one will notice an extra backpack in the bunch."

His costume wasn't bad. In fact, Turkey looked just like a backpack . . .

. . . almost.

"*Tote-ally* foolish, Turkey!" said Max. "Critters aren't allowed at school.
Pack it up and head back to the farm!"

"Gobble, gobble," moaned Turkey. "I've got to find a way in!"

Rooster peeked in the window.
"They're starting story time.

"A book disguise might just **doodle-doodle-doo**," he said.

Turkey agreed.

His costume wasn't bad. In fact, Turkey looked just like a book . . . almost.

"We'll create a little distraction out here
while you **book** it inside," said Sheep.

Turkey stayed quiet and still during the story.

"Can we read that one next?" asked a girl, pointing right at Turkey.

The teacher looked. "That's no book! Turkey, I'm *page-ing* the principal.

"Critters aren't allowed at school! You're **bound** for the farm!"

Turkey bolted outside. "Gobble, gobble!" he howled.
"I need a better disguise."

"It's almost *r-e-e-cess*," said Horse.
"Maybe it's a good chance to blend in with the group."

"Score!" said Turkey. "A ball is sure to get in the game."

His costume wasn't bad. In fact, Turkey looked just like a soccer ball . . .

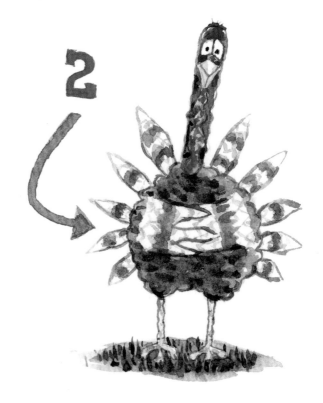

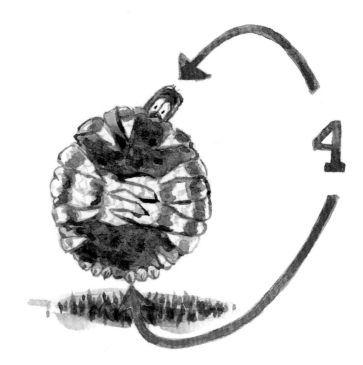

. . . almost.

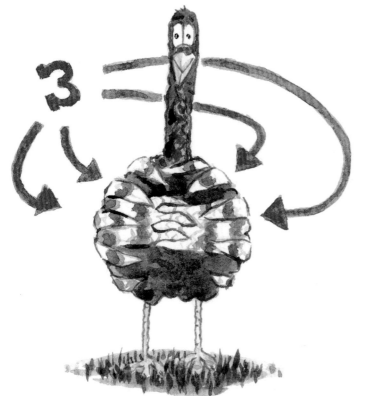

The kids came running out to the playground.
Horse bucked Turkey up in the air . . .

and Cow head-butted him
into the middle of the crowd.

"GOAL!"

"Cool—jumbo soccer!" cried a boy.

Turkey was dizzy and dinged. He teetered and tottered—right into Millie.

"I call a *fowl*!" cried Millie. "Turkeys aren't allowed at school!
Roll on home!"

"Gobble, gobble, gobble," grumbled Turkey. "How am I ever going to get inside?"

"Maybe you can make your **mooo-ve** as a lunch lady
in the **calf-eteria**," said Cow.

"Brilliant!" said Turkey.

His costume wasn't bad. In fact, Turkey looked just like a lunch lady . . . almost.

Pig pilfered a cart filled with food. Turkey pushed it right into the serving line and began to parcel out pizza.

"*Cheez* Turkey!" hollered the head lunch lady. "No one is *swallowing* that disguise. Critters aren't allowed at school.

Out . . . out . . . **out!**"

The sign reads:

Farm Days This Week!

Turkey trudged outside.

"I just don't get it," squawked Rooster. "It's 'Farm Days.'
We should be front and center."

"That's it!" cried Turkey. "I have the perfect plan!"

The principal poked her head in the classroom.

"You have special guest visitors for 'Farm Days,'" she said.
"Farmer Jake and his animals are going to sing a song with you."

Turkey and his pals walked to the front of the classroom.

Turkey sang out, "Farmer Jake, he had a farm. E-I-E-I-O.
And on that farm he had a ... TURKEY. E-I-E-I-O."

The children cheered. "Can we sing some more?" Millie asked.

She looked at the teacher hopefully. So did Turkey and his pals.

"Critters still aren't allowed at school . . . but I suppose
they can be our special farm guests this afternoon."

So Turkey and his pals stayed.
And it was a **FARM-TASTIC** first—and last—day of school!